Hawk Davidson

Mystery at
Desert Lake

Tony Reno

High Noon Books
Novato, California

Editor: Jim Arena
Cover Art: Jim McConnell
Cover Design: Bonnie Gatter
Illustrations: Jim McConnell

International Standard Book Number: 1-57128-327-7

14 13 12 11 10 09 08 07 06 05
10 09 08 07 06 05 04 03 02 01

Contents

The Town of Desert Lake

CHAPTER 1

All Terrain

Hawk Davidson worked for ACME Extreme Sports. He tested extreme sports gear. Today Hawk was racing ATVs (All Terrain Vehicles). The race was on an outdoor track close to the ACME building. ACME's main competitor, RIVAL Sports, also had riders in the race.

Hawk had made it through the first three races. Now there were only four riders left. It was the final race of the day. Two of the riders.had a RIVAL logo on their shirts.

Hawk did not know who the other rider was. He had a Number 14 on his shirt. He rode a special model. It could be driven with hand controls.

Hawk started the engine of the ACME 650cc Destroyer. Number 14 turned his helmet. He looked at Hawk and gave him the 'thumbs-up' sign. Hawk nodded back with his helmet. He wished he knew who this guy was. But he could not see the face of Number 14. It was hidden by his helmet and racing goggles.

But Hawk had other things to worry about. He had only ridden this a track a few times. He knew the track was harder than it looked.

The horn sounded and the four riders took

off. Mud and dirt flew everywhere. Number 14 and one of the RIVAL riders took the lead. The other rider stayed behind Hawk.

The track began with three large bumps. These were no problem for the riders. Then they all went into a left turn and prepared for the rough part of the track. Hawk could feel the shocks on his ATV as it hit the track.

Then came two sharp turns. Number 14 was still in the lead. One RIVAL rider rode right next to him. The two ATVs hit each other as they took the first turn.

Just then Hawk's ATV was bumped by the second RIVAL rider. Hawk bumped the rider back. He gunned the engine through the two turns. He was still in third place. But now the first RIVAL rider was in the lead.

The next part of the track was 100 feet of water and mud. All the riders slowed down. The ATVs sunk into the slick track. Hawk felt another hit. It was from the RIVAL rider behind him. Hawk kept his ATV from sliding out of control.

Should have known these RIVAL riders don't play fair, thought Hawk.

Hawk slammed on his brakes and held on. The RIVAL rider yelled. He turned to avoid Hawk's ATV, but he turned too sharp and skidded. He ran off into the brush on the side of the track. The second RIVAL rider was out of the race.

Hawk now looked ahead. The last part of the course had several small jumps through trees. It ended with a sprint to the finish line. The RIVAL rider and Number 14 were taking the jumps. They were battling for the lead. Hawk saw them bump each other a few times.

Hawk was slowly gaining. But he was still a full 20 feet behind. Then Number 14 made a move and passed the RIVAL rider. It looked like Number 14 was going to win the race. But then Number 14 slowed down. He stayed in front of the RIVAL rider.

What's he doing? thought Hawk. He was now ten feet from the other riders.

The RIVAL rider tried to pass. But

Number 14 quickly turned his ATV and stayed in front. Hawk was now next to the two riders. Then Number 14 sped up.

"You're on your own, Hawk," said Number 14.

All riders were now speeding to the finish line. The RIVAL rider made a move. But Hawk stayed ahead of him. Number 14 crossed the finish line first. Hawk was second and the RIVAL rider third. Number 14 kept his helmet on and rode away.

"Who was that guy?" Hawk said to himself.

CHAPTER 2

Hello, Old Friend

Hawk drove his ATV next to Number 14. The rider still had his helmet on. Hawk was about to say something, when Number 14 turned around.

"It's good to see you again, Hawk," Number 14 said. "Do you know who I am?"

"You're the guy who just kicked my tail in the race," Hawk said.

The rider laughed. "It's Jack – Jack Kelly."

"Jack?! I can't believe it. It *is* you. You sure fooled me," Hawk said. "How are you doing? I haven't seen you in a few years."

"I'm doing fine," Jack said. "But my home town isn't. I live in a town next to a lake. It is in the middle of a desert. The town is called Desert Lake. It's a great place for riding ATV's, kayaking, river-rafting, jet-skiing..."

"Sounds great," said Hawk. "So what's wrong?"

Jack said, "Desert Lake needs the water that comes down from the mountains. It goes through the desert canyon and into the lake by the town. Less and less water is flowing into the lake. It's bad for the town of Desert Lake. It is also bad for the desert."

"What can I do?" Hawk asked.

"I could use your help. I want to search the mountain and the river canyon. We'll need ATVs to do that. And since you ride ATVs…"

Hawk laughed. Jack was still the same joker he was when they were kids.

"I get it. I have some free time until the ATV race next weekend," Hawk said. "I can be there tomorrow."

"Great!" said Jack. "The airport is next to the town. I'll meet you there on my ATV. There will be an extra ATV waiting for you."

"See you later," said Hawk. He then pulled out his cell phone. He called Mick at ACME Sports. Mick was ACME's mechanic. Mick also knew how to fly airplanes and helicopters.

"This is Mick," said Mick.

"Hey Mick, it's Hawk. Do you think you could give me a ride in ACME's plane? I need to get to Desert Lake Airport."

"I know where that is," Mick said. "I'll be glad to give you a ride. Just make sure you are back for the next race. The ACME Bosses would be very upset if you missed it."

CHAPTER 3

The Next Day

Hawk looked out the window of the plane. They were near Desert Lake Airport. He could see a few dozen houses and a lake several miles away.

A river ran to the lake. The river came from a series of nearby mountains. The river bed looked large. But it did not seem like there was much water flowing down the river into Desert Lake.

The plane circled Desert Lake Airport. Mick prepared to land. Hawk had just told Mick what Jack Kelly said about Desert Lake.

"Take care of yourself, Hawk. You don't know what's going on out there. There could be more trouble than you think," Mick said.

"Aren't I always careful?" Hawk asked with a grin.

"Check your supplies," Mick said.

"I'll check them one more time if that makes you happy," Hawk said. He looked inside his backpack. There were five Power Bars, a bag of trail mix, a compass, lighter, watch, lantern, and cell phone. There were also two RIVAL Spring Mountain water bottles.

"What the heck is this!" said Hawk. "This has to be a bad dream."

"Oh, are you talking about the bottled water?" Mick asked. "It was only water I could get on such short notice."

"But we work for ACME Sports," Hawk said. "ACME Sport's main competitor is RIVAL Sports. And now they are making bottled water. I can't drink this stuff."

"I dislike them as much as you do, and I know the owner." Mick then lowered the landing gear. He guided the plane onto the Desert Lake Airport runway.

The plane rolled to a stop. Hawk stepped off and waved to Mick. "See you tomorrow," he said.

Hawk then watched Mick take off. The

sound of the plane faded. He then heard the sound of an approaching ATV. It was his friend Jack.

"Get on, Hawk. I've got an ATV for you on the other side of the airport," said Jack. "We will ride out to Desert Lake. We can have some fun on the way."

Hawk got on his ATV and put on his helmet. A flat air-raft and pump was attached to the back of the ATV. There was also a kayak and paddle.

"Could you hand me that kayak?" Jack asked.

"Sure," said Hawk. "Why the extra gear?"

"I kayak when I'm not riding my ATV. The river was once a great place for kayaking. That was before it started to dry up," said Jack.

He hooked the kayak onto his ATV.

"When did this happen?" asked Hawk.

"About six months ago," said Jack.

"I'll tell you all about it when we get back to Desert Lake. I know a great trail to take. Follow me if you can," Jack said as he roared off.

"Hey, don't get too far ahead. You know the desert much better than I do," Hawk said. "I would hate to get lost out here."

CHAPTER 4

Desert Lake

It was afternoon when Hawk and Jack rode into Desert Lake. The town was at the base of a long mountain range. It ran along the desert as far as the eye could see. A river of fresh water ran from the top of the mountain range into the lake.

"Not much water going down the river," Hawk said.

"There should be enough water to go river rafting," Jack said. "That's why I'm hoping you can help me…"

"Take a look at the river," Jack said. "It's more like a stream. There's barely enough water to ride a kayak."

Hawk nodded and Jack went on, "If the river and lake dries up, there's no boating and kayaking. If there's no kayaking, fewer people will want to stay at the hotel. If fewer people stay at the hotel, no one will eat at the diners. If no one eats at the diners…"

Hawk spoke up, "Then no one visits Desert Lake. Then the people living here will have to leave."

"You got it," said Jack.

Just then Hawk saw something.

"What's that out there?" Hawk asked. He

pointed out into the desert. Two riders were heading quickly away from town.

"Looks like the same riders that we beat in the race the other day," said Jack.

Hawk started his ATV and turned to Jack, "I'm going to find out."

"I hate it when he does that," Jack said to himself. He started his ATV.

The two ATV riders now looked like two small dots. If these were the same riders from the race, Hawk was sure he could catch up to them. Hawk gunned his engine. He kept his eye on the two dots in the distance.

Hawk then saw another ATV next to his. Jack turned to Hawk and gave him the 'thumbs-up' sign.

The two riders kept riding. They headed into the middle of the desert. After 20 minutes, they were still far away. But Hawk and Jack were slowly gaining. Hawk thought he saw one rider turn and look back at them.

"They know we're after them," said Hawk.

The two RIVAL riders then split up. They headed in two different directions.

"You take that one," Hawk said.

"Right," said Jack, "But I'm turning back in 15 minutes. You should, too. The sun is going down."

"I'll meet you back at Desert Lake by sunset," Hawk said.

CHAPTER 5

Into the Desert

Hawk was now just behind the rider, but he was starting to worry. He had been after the rider for 40 minutes. Hawk guessed that he had gone at least 15 miles. The sun was going down and they were in the middle of the desert. The rider was flying over a group of small sand dunes. Hawk stayed on them, but thought about turning back.

Just then Hawk saw the rider make a sharp turn. He could not see the rider any more. Hawk continued to cruise forward. He drove up to the top of one of the hills and looked around. He could not see or hear the other ATV.

"Something's wrong," Hawk said out loud.

Hawk drove around the top of one of the higher dunes and looked around.

I'm turning back, Hawk thought to himself.

As Hawk began to speed up he heard an engine. As he turned to look, his ATV was hit from behind. Hawk flew off his bike. His ATV flew forward down the dune and hit front first. Smoke was pouring out.

It was the RIVAL rider! He then drove his ATV to the top of one of the hills.

"Go back to Desert Lake, Hawk. The sun is about to go down." The rider spoke in a deep

Hawk flew off his bike. His ATV flew forward down the dune and hit front first.

voice. Then he sped off toward the mountains.

Hawk walked back to his ATV. The front end was crushed and the drive shaft was damaged. The ATV could not be ridden.

Hawk then looked in his pack. He took out his cell phone. He tried to call Jack, but his phone was too far out of range.

He then took out a bottle of Rival Spring Mountain Water and took a drink. He was too far out to see the town or the lake. He could only see the mountains next to the town. That was where the RIVAL rider had gone.

It was too late to do anything now. Hawk found some shelter under a rock and went to sleep.

CHAPTER 6

Walking

Might as well keep after that rider, Hawk thought. The next morning Hawk began to walk. He hoped that Jack would come looking for him. He could follow his trail toward the mountain. Hawk knew that fresh water came down this main river into Desert Lake. But there were other small rivers that also came down the mountain.

He could feel the desert heat. As he walked he reached into his pack. He grabbed some of the trail mix. He then opened his last

24

bottle of Rival Spring Mountain Water.

Hawk had to admit the water tasted good. It was too bad it came from RIVAL Sports. They were the enemy. That's why he had gone to work for ACME Sports. Both ACME and RIVAL made sports gear. Hawk liked all extreme sports. But he didn't like RIVAL. RIVAL Sports was as ruthless as could be. ACME Sports was, well, it was a company that was not RIVAL. ACME vs. RIVAL.

Hawk had been walking for several miles. He saw that the mountain was farther away than he thought. The rivers he had seen from his wrecked ATV were dry.

Hawk guessed that it was around noon. The sun was high above him. He also guessed that it was well over 100 degrees. Hawk began to wonder if he should have headed back to town.

After three hours Hawk reached the base of the mountain. He looked up to the top. Hawk could see some small bushes up there. He hoped that meant there was water close by. But there was still a few thousand feet of climbing to go.

Hawk rested for a while. He reached into his pack for some more trail mix. He wished he had another bottle of Rival Spring Mountain Water. Hawk spotted a small trail. It headed up the mountain.

CHAPTER 7

The Grey Man

It was now about four o'clock. It had been a few hours since Hawk had any water. The heat was getting to Hawk. He felt dizzy and weak.

He had reached the bushes near the top of the mountain. But still no water.

Was Jack looking for him now? Just then he thought he heard the sound of an ATV. It came from farther up the mountain. And what about Mick? Would he see the broken ATV from his plane? Would Mick even know it was Hawk's ATV?

Hawk started to climb again. He heard another sound of an ATV. There was something coming out of the bushes. Hawk tried to run and hide. But he was too tired and moved too slow.

"Jack, is that you?" Hawk shouted into the trees.

"Not even close," said a voice.

"Who are you?" Hawk asked. He could now see the person on the ATV. It was a man in a plain grey suit. He carried a briefcase.

"Have you ever wanted to travel all over the world, Hawk? Use the best gear on the best courses? Would you like to make lots of money?"

"Well, I've thought about it..." Hawk said.

"Then I'm someone who can change your

life for the better. A guy with your talent should have the best. I can give it to you," the man said. He pulled out a stack of papers. "All you have to do is sign here, here, and here."

Hawk stared at the man for a few seconds. "Who do you work for" Hawk asked.

"What does it matter, Hawk? I can offer you a chance to have it all. What more could you want?"

"Got any water?" Hawk asked.

"Why, Hawk? You're so close."

"Close to what? How did you get here on that ATV?" Hawk asked again.

"Someone's watching you, Hawk. Gotta go. We'll meet again." The Grey Man rode off into the trees.

CHAPTER 8

At the Top

Hawk was too weary to run after the man. Instead he climbed the last few hundred feet to the top of the mountain. Hawk could hear a river flowing nearby.

"Finally!" shouted Hawk. "Fresh water!"

"What was that!?" a voice said.

"I'll check it out," said another.

Hawk heard an ATV coming closer. He ducked into some small bushes. He saw a rider wearing a helmet coming his way. Hawk waited until it passed right beside him. Then, with all his strength, he leapt onto the ATV.

The ATV driver let out a yell. He was taken by surprise by Hawk. The two tumbled away from the ATV. It drove off the trail and stopped in a ditch. The ATV's motor kept running. Hawk wrestled with the rider. He got his weight around so that he had the rider pinned to the ground.

"OK, OK, Hawk, take it easy," said a familiar voice.

"What?" said Hawk.

"We've only got a little time. I have to get back. It's a good thing the motor is running on that ATV. They can't hear us talking..."

"Sam?" Hawk asked.

The rider took off her helmet. Long hair tumbled out. Hawk was surprised. He was relieved to see his friend and main rival looking up at him.

"That's right, it's me," said Sam, "Why are you looking at me like that?"

"Now I know it was you that we raced against yesterday," said Hawk.

"So what, Hawk? I work for RIVAL. I can't go easy on you. I didn't want you to know it was me. You would have thought twice about running me off the road in that race."

"Maybe, maybe not," Hawk said. "But that doesn't explain why you busted up my ATV. Or

32

why you made me walk all the way up here!"

"Calm down Hawk. I was trying to help you. I didn't want you to come. There is danger here. Get on the ATV and I'll give you a ride."

"To get some water, I hope."

Sam got on the ATV and Hawk got on back. Sam rode along the top of the mountain. They rode toward the main river that cut through the top of the mountain.

"The main river heads right down to Desert Lake. It still has running water, but it won't for long. But why bother with the river when you can drink this?" From the ATV, Sam pulled out a nice cold bottle of RIVAL Spring Mountain Water.

"What are you doing?" Hawk asked. "Why drink that when the river is right here?"

"Hawk, could you do me a favor and look over there," Sam said. She pointed to some trees.

"Sam, I'm really thirsty. Stop playing games." But Hawk turned around anyway. He couldn't believe his eyes. Behind some trees he could see a sign. It read: <u>RIVAL Spring Mountain Water Dam. Do Not Trespass.</u>

Behind some trees he could see a sign. It read: RIVAL
Spring Mountain Water Dam: Do not Trespass

CHAPTER 9

When the Levee Breaks

"So this is the answer to everything," Hawk said as he stood next to the sign and looked at the dam. It was large enough to hold hundreds of thousands of gallons of water.

"You mean why the river to Desert Lake is drying up?" Sam asked.

"Yes, and why this RIVAL water tastes so good," Hawk said as he took of a sip of Sam's water.

"Hawk, I have to go back. I won't tell

them I saw you. Just follow the river for a few miles and you will find yourself back at Desert Lake."

"Are those some kayaks over there?" Hawk asked.

"Yes. Somebody brought them to kayak around the dam," Sam said. "Too bad there's no time to have some fun. Gotta go, Hawk. Take care."

"That's much better," Hawk said as he finished drinking the bottle of RIVAL water.

Sam rode back the way she came. Hawk then ran toward the kayaks. They looked like they were in good shape. He then went to a small control box next to the dam. There were four buttons on it. Hawk pressed the one that said "OPEN." He then heard the sound of motors. The doors of the dam began to slowly move. Water began spilling down into the river.

Hawk put the kayak in the dam and got in. Kayaking wasn't Hawk's best sport. He could see it was the fastest way down. Hawk paddled toward the doors. They were now half open. Water was now pouring into the river. Hawk knew he should have stopped the doors at this point. But it was too late. He was in the kayak and on his way.

Thousands of gallons of water now fell into the river. Hawk got ready as he was sucked into the stream. His kayak crashed into the river.

Hawk could barely keep control. The force of the river rapids shot water everywhere. Currents made waves that slammed into the rocks.

Hawk tried to take a look ahead to see what was coming. Then he saw two RIVAL riders. They were now about 15 feet behind him. They were also in kayaks.

"You're not getting down from this mountain, Hawk. You know too much," one rider shouted.

Hawk was about to shout something back. Then he saw another kayak drop down behind the RIVAL riders. He then gave a 'thumbs-up' sign to Hawk.

"It's Jack!" Hawk shouted to himself.

Jack Kelly closed in on the two RIVAL riders. He shocked the first one by bumping him from behind. The RIVAL kayaker yelled out. He tried to keep control of his kayak. Jack and the kayaker kept fighting.

The second RIVAL rider shot forward away from Jack and ran into Hawk. Hawk's kayak spun around. He stared at the second rider.

"Now it's payback time for the ATV race the other day. Good-bye, Hawk," the second rider shouted.

He was about to ram Hawk when a loud roar rose right above them.

"That's got to be Mick!" Hawk shouted.

The second RIVAL rider looked up. He

lost control of his kayak and crashed into Hawk. Hawk tried to control his own kayak. Then Jack and the other RIVAL kayak crashed into Hawk.

All four kayaks were now tangled together and spinning down the river.

"Get ready, Hawk. We're going for a little ride!" shouted Jack.

Hawk looked around. He could see Desert Lake below. He also saw that the force of the river had made a 50 foot waterfall down to the lake.

There was nothing they could do. The kayaks tumbled down the waterfall. They landed with a huge crash in Desert Lake.

"Get ready, Hawk. We're going for a little ride!"
shouted Jack.

CHAPTER 10

Back at Desert Lake

Mick and the police were waiting by the shore. They picked up the RIVAL kayakers. Mick helped pull Hawk out of Desert Lake.

Mick and Hawk quickly helped pull Jack out of the lake. Jack Kelly was such a good athlete that Hawk almost forgot he could not use his legs.

"Thanks, guys!" Jack said, "And thanks for helping me solve the mystery of Desert Lake. RIVAL had dammed the river. Maybe now things will get back to normal. People can have some fun around here again."

"Looks like the cops and I came just in time," Mick said. He turned to Hawk. "It's a good thing Jack called me when you didn't return last night. When I was flying here, I saw your ATV wreck. I could also see your trail into the mountain."

"So that was you in the plane..." Hawk said.

"We better get going, Hawk, or the ACME Bosses will get angry." Mick said. "By the way, I'm thirsty. Do you have any more of that bottled water?"

Hawk and Jack just looked at each other and smiled.